# Second Chance

# Second Chance

A NOVEL BY
## SYD BANKS

Duval-Bibb Publishing Co.
Tampa

*Second Chance*

*Published by Duval-Bibb Publishing Co.*

*Copyright © 1983, 1987, 1989 by Syd Banks*

*All rights reserved.*

*Published in the United States by Duval-Bibb Publishing Co.*

*Originally published by Med-Psych Publications.*

*Second Edition*


*Cover Photo:       Syd Banks*

*Cover Design:     Richard Mayer*


*Printed in the United States of America*

*First Duval-Bibb Publishing Co. edition: July 1989*

*97 96 95 94 93 92 91 90 89    10 9 8 7 6 5 4 3 2*

**Library of Congress Cataloging-in-Publication Data**

*Banks, Syd R., 1931 -*
    *Second chance : a novel / by Syd Banks. -- 1st Duval Bibb*
    *Pub. Co. ed.*
        *p.   cm.*
    *"Originally published by Med-Psych Publications"--CIP verso*
    *t.p.*
    *ISBN 0-937713-01-5 : $10.95 -- ISBN 0-937713-04-X (trade*
    *pbk.) : $6.95*
    *I. Title.*
    *PS3552.A494S4   1989*
    *813'.54--dc20*                                    *89-50501*
                                                            *CIP*

For additional copies or bulk orders, contact:

**Duval-Bibb Publishing Co.**
P.O. Box 23704
Tampa, Florida 33623 U.S.A.

iv       (813) 870-1970

## <u>Dedication</u>

*To humanity, in the hope that this book may help alleviate some of the needless suffering.*

*Second Chance*

**A**t some time in your life, you may come upon a book which strikes a long forgotten inner chord, bringing back beautiful feelings that have been lost in time - a fascinating book, one you will never forget. You hold in your hands such a book.

Set on the beautiful Hawaiian island of Maui, "Second Chance" takes the reader on a mystical journey into a world of soft tropical breezes, rainbows arching gently over crystal blue oceans, and mysteries revealed beneath diamond studded skies.

It is a fictional story about a successful young New York executive, who comes to the Hawaiian Islands to seek solace from the shock and despair of losing his wife, and learning his own life is threatened by terminal cancer.

Here, an intriguing gentleman with an unusual sense of humor, and an exceptional understanding of life, introduces him to an enigmatic elderly Hawaiian woman known as Mamma Lila. She is a lady of great wisdom and compassion who speaks in riddles that mystify the intellect, but touch the soul.

She tells the young man of powers that can help him rise above his predicament, taking him to a reality beyond anything he has ever known.

# Second Chance

# CHAPTER 1

IT was exactly two months ago that I arrived for the first time at the Maui airport. Like many others I was seeking some rest, some sun and some time to evaluate my life, which at this point was shattered. My wife had died after two brief years of marriage. Three months later I was told by my doctors that I had an inoperable, malignant tumor at the base of my spine. My nerves were completely frayed, and I was the perfect candidate for a nervous breakdown.

I was loaded with pills. I had pills for pain, pills for nervous tension, pills for sleeping and pills to help me

3

Second
Chance

forget the existing horrors of my life—"anti-depressants" they were called. The pain pills eased the pain temporarily, but nothing it seemed could stop the blind panic or stop me from asking, "Why? Why me?"

I had been advised to try a therapy group, and although I had read all about the various therapies they hadn't helped me. I tried Gestalt but the panic continued. "There's a better answer," someone said. "Try meditation." There seemed to be an abundance of ideas and techniques to try, yet I failed to find any answer to my problems. Perhaps there wasn't an answer for someone in my predicament.

How well I remember my first glimmer of beautiful Maui; the shapely Hawaiian girls greeting us with flower leis and the melodious "Aloha." Outside the airport I stood surrounded by hedges of pink bougainvillea. Stately palms swayed gently in the warm breeze and flowers were in brilliant color everywhere. I took a deep breath of the soft Maui air then headed towards the hotel courtesy bus. From there it was a twenty-five minute drive to my hotel where once again I was greeted with warm hospitality. "Hang loose," said a large Hawaiian porter. "You are in Hawaii so hang loose and leave your problems behind." "How wonderful," I thought, "if it were really that simple."

After I was given directions at the front desk, I found my room tastefully decorated in Hawaiian decor. Behind me was the golf course, and in front lay a wide expanse of well kept lawn dotted with palm trees. A view of turquoise water and couples enjoying themselves by the pool suddenly brought a feeling of loneliness, and I no longer saw the beauty. The old feelings and thoughts were back in my head. "Why me?"

A pain shot through my spine. I stiffened and automatically reached for my pills to ease the pain. I wasn't hungry, so after a hot shower I took a sleeping pill and climbed into bed. Soon I was drifting off.

I awoke the next morning with a feeling of disappointment. Hawaii was not what I had hoped it would be. It did not possess the tranquility that I had expected. It had not helped me in any way with my problems; I still felt the way I had at home. I wondered if there was any such thing as a resting place in this world.

I got up and decided to spend my first day on the grounds of the hotel. I lay in the sun by the pool for a while, watched the people and walked around exploring the surroundings. About four o'clock I began to feel restless and bored. I had been told that Lahaina was a unique little town well worth seeing, so I decided to rent a car and visit it myself.

The drive into Lahaina had some incredible scenery but my mind was so busy I couldn't appreciate it. Once again, my disappointment in Hawaii swept over me.

# Second Chance

I turned the corner to find a sign in front of me that said LAHAINA—3 miles. As if a bolt of lightning had struck me, my whole body suddenly felt electrified. Every fiber of my being tingled. I felt a tremendous force pulling me towards some unknown destination in Lahaina. Something was happening to me that I had never experienced before. It was exciting and at the same time frightening as my mind struggled to assess my emotions. As I entered the town the force became undeniably stronger.

I parked my car by a magnificent banyan tree that looked as if it had been weathered by years of time. Across the road I could see a charming old turn-of-the century building, commanding a view of the ocean.

The Pioneer Inn, I was told, had quite a historic background. As I gazed, entranced by the scene around me, I felt a sense of peace come over me. I turned and began wandering down the picturesque street past quaint old-fashioned stores. A little cafe overlooking the harbour caught my eye and I decided to investigate. "The Crow's Nest" had a distinctive tropical atmosphere—perched above the sea, open to the air on three sides, little birds flying through, stopping here and there for crumbs.

A beautiful blond waitress with a golden tan came towards me. As she took my order, we began to discuss Lahaina. She explained how Lahaina had grown from a small settlement to a world-renowned port-of-call for the then vast whaling fleets. Sailors of many nations regarded it as Paradise. Her conversation was filled with interesting and humorous anecdotes.

I finished my refreshments and decided to continue my exploration of Lahaina. I walked down the steps and onto the street. I stood there for a moment, and once again I felt myself being pulled in the direction of the Pioneer Inn by some unknown force. My whole body vibrated. The hairs on my neck felt electrified, my heart pounded and I felt breathless. It was the same feeling I had had earlier and one that I could not explain, yet it was as tangible as the sidewalk I stood on.

I approached the Pioneer Inn and noticed an old stone wall in front of the library's green lawn. A few people sat on the wall meditating, others sat under palm trees, and still others stood looking seaward at the sunset.

In front of me lay an incredible vista of sailboats silhouetted in the setting sun. A golden path cut across the blue water, high-lighting the last of the day's surfers approaching home with the incoming waves. A stillness seemed to pervade. Out of no-where, the gentle whisper of the evening trade winds seemed to caress everything around me.

In the midst of this scene a man appeared and walked slowly to the wall. He was about five foot-eight inches, clean shaven, and had black hair. In the gathering twilight it was difficult to judge his age. His face was free of lines and his body youthful and supple.

I felt inexplicably drawn towards this person, so I walked over and sat down beside him. There was a quality of strength, a presence, that emanated from him. He turned towards me, his smiling blue eyes holding mine for a moment, then his gaze returned to the sunset.

After the sun had set, people quietly began to talk. I felt a deep tranquility. I turned to the gentleman beside me, feeling, for no reason at all, that he was someone I could talk to. All at once it began to pour out of me; all my new experiences that day, all the problems I had, what I had been feeling and now this tremendous tranquility that I hadn't experienced since I was a child. He sat listening patiently.

I explained that I was vice-president of a furniture manufacturing corporation, based in New York. At the age of twenty-nine, I was financially stable, owned my own home but I still felt a failure. Added to my problems was the fact that I had just found out I had an inoperable tumor at the base of my spine. I felt the world had definitely been cruel to me and I couldn't help asking myself "Why me?"

Looking deep into my eyes, the stranger began to speak. "Why not look at it this way? There is no such thing as a failure. Surely failure is only in the eyes of the beholder and the more the belief exists the more the so-called failure will be. Don't you see, it is the thought that is the seed, the failure is the form. Without the thought it is virtually impossible to be a failure."

His words created an excitement within me though I didn't understand what he had said. I felt relief wash over me as the stranger spoke again.

"It appears to me that you have no hope, but one should never feel hopeless because there is an answer to everything."

I sat speechless, not knowing what to say. Finally I gathered my bearings and inquired, "How can you say there is an answer to everything when I am sitting here now with an inoperable, malignant tumor at the base of my spine? I have tried three different specialists and the prognosis is that I have from six months to two years to live. As my condition deteriorates I will gradually become crippled and ultimately bedridden with a great deal of pain. How can there possibly be an answer to *this*?"

He gazed at me with total compassion on his face and answered, "The trouble is you see this world as the only reality that exists. You have trapped yourself on a level of consciousness. You must learn to take the limitations off life and see there are more realities than meet the eye."

The man's words took me by surprise. It was not the

kind of answer I expected nor had I ever heard such an incredible statement. I sat utterly speechless for a moment then I replied, "What you just said does not make any sense to me. It just doesn't make sense!"

His eyes twinkled. "I didn't expect it would," he replied.

Normally I would have felt angry and insulted by such a statement but his honesty was so straightforward that I found myself smiling. We sat in silence for a while, then I inquired, "What is your idea of success?"

He looked out to sea as if he were pondering. "Simple," he said. "Happiness and contentment."

I waited patiently for him to expound on his theory but he just sat there.

"Is that all?" I inquired, "Just happiness and contentment."

"Yes," he replied.

I was about to inquire further into his philosophy, as I had a dozen questions stirring in my mind, but he rose, touched my shoulder gently with his hand and said, "I must leave now, but we will meet again." With that he turned and walked away.

I sat watching the last color of the sunset fade, then I got up and walked towards my car. As I was driving home I realized I didn't even know the stranger's name, nor had I told him mine. I wondered if I really would see him again.

*Second Chance*

His words had stirred me, and in my head I kept hearing over and over again, "There is an answer to everything."

It was not only his words that captivated me but the conviction with which he said them. A feeling of joy came over me and tears ran down my cheeks. Perhaps there was hope, of which the stranger had spoken.

# CHAPTER 2

ACOUPLE of days passed since my meeting with the unusual stranger. I had spent them close to my hotel as I found I couldn't stay in any one position very long without pain. Tonight, however, I felt the urge to venture into Lahaina. I hoped to see the stranger again and perhaps have another interesting conversation with him.

When I arrived in the little village of Lahaina, the sun was a huge ball of red fire sitting on the sea. There was no breeze. It was very warm and still. I looked around but saw no sign of the man I was looking for. A feeling of disappointment swept over me, and I began to chastise myself for being so foolish. What was I doing running around looking for someone about whom I knew absolutely nothing? It was an absurd situation.

At that moment I felt someone touch my shoulder from behind and I heard a cheerful "Aloha." Turning, I looked into the eyes of the man I sought.

"You know," I said, "I realized when you left the other night that although I had told you my whole life history, I didn't even know your name, nor had I told you mine." Extending my hand I said, "My name is Richard Sullivan." He clasped mine firmly and said, "I'm Jonathan Davies."

The sun had now slipped into the sea leaving pastel color over the sky, the sea and the land. The fleeting twilight was pink and the whole sky seemed to be alive. Perhaps this was the "Maui magic" I had heard people speak of.

I asked Jonathan if he would like to join me for dinner at the Pioneer Inn. "I'd love to," he said. We walked into the rotunda of the Inn and I had the feeling of going back in time. I thought of all the life this hotel must have seen. It certainly was a unique place.

The hostess ushered us through the rotunda to a courtyard. I was surprised to see a swimming pool with turquoise water reflecting the light of tiki torches and a gazebo surrounded by gently swaying palms. The sky was clear and dotted with a thousand stars.

There was a sense of great beauty, almost of unreality about the place.

When we were seated, I told Jonathan that our meeting the other night had been a remarkable experience for me and that although I found his philosophy difficult to comprehend, I had been intrigued. I went on to tell him that I had never felt such extreme emotions as I had since our meeting.

He listened attentively to what I was saying, then he said, "Don't try to figure it out. Just enjoy your vacation and your good newfound feelings."

"I'm afraid I am a very inquisitive person," I said, "and I am intrigued by the events of the other evening."

"Don't you know what curiosity did to the cat?" Jonathan asked with a chuckle, as if he knew something I didn't. "Had you been able to SEE you would have found the answer you sought. It was right before your eyes."

"What do you mean I couldn't SEE?" I asked.

"I can't tell you what I mean by SEEING," Jonathan replied. "It is something you must experience for yourself. The other night for instance, when you were sitting on the wall looking at the sunset, the presence of *true* knowledge was all around you. The beautiful *feelings* you had were related to the amount of knowledge you absorbed. However, had you SEEN, you most certainly would not be asking me this question.

# *Second Chance*

SEEING is an experience of going beyond the intellectual capabilities to which you now limit yourself."

I felt somewhat insulted by his words and assured him that I thought my intelligence was equal to his; that after graduating and having gone on to get my Master's degree in Administration, I felt capable of understanding his definition of SEEING.

He looked at me intently for a moment, shook his head, and replied, "You are talking about intellectual intelligence, are you not?"

"Yes, of course," I answered.

"How wonderful," he said, "if it were that simple, but it isn't. One can't just memorize and understand. What I am trying to tell you doesn't lend itself to mankind's way of thinking intellectually. Remember, I told you the other evening that there are more realities than meet the eye. This SEEING must come from an experience of SEEING another reality."

There was a long pause as my mind scrambled for a foothold. For years I had been proud of my ability to fence verbally with people. Now I felt I had come upon an opponent, who managed to confuse me in a manner so unorthodox that my intellectual logic couldn't cope. I felt my ego badly bruised. This man sitting across the table from me was so different, a tremor of fear ran all the way through me. I had never had a conversation with anyone who made me feel this way. It was very disconcerting and I didn't under-

*Second Chance*

stand why.

He seemed to sense my confusion and said, "Listen, my friend. For some unknown reason you and I have crossed paths in this life. We have encountered each other. Call it fate or whatever you wish. When I first saw you, I took a liking to you. I could SEE you wanted someone to talk to; so here we are sitting in this beautiful restaurant. Let's just enjoy this evening."

We both smiled as the atmosphere changed from one of intensity to one of lightheartedness.

"Have you always lived in Hawaii?" I asked Jonathan.

"No," he replied, "but I feel it is my home. I've been here about ten years. I was born and raised on a small farm in Arizona with my three brothers and two sisters.

"After the second world war I met and married my late wife. Right after our marriage we moved to Alabama where we had two children, Brian and Craig. Brian is now a practicing physician in Baltimore and Craig still lives in Alabama where he teaches school."

The waiter arrived with the wine list. I asked Jonathan if he had any preference. He shook his head and said, "No, thanks. Alcohol makes my head fuzzy. I don't like the taste of it so I don't drink."

I was reluctant to take alcohol while on medication so I declined as well. I felt very comfortable and relaxed. It was a beautiful restaurant and the food was delicious.

"It's good to see you starting to relax," Jonathan said. "As they say in Hawaii, 'Hang loose'."

"That's a nice expression. I like it." I replied.

We sat looking at the other tourists, enjoying the holiday feeling that was present.

After a while Jonathan turned to me and began speaking, "You know, Richard, what you have to do, is find out what MIND *is*, then you will know how to solve your problems."

I stared at him in disbelief. "That is the most astounding theory I have ever heard in my life," I answered.

"It is not a theory," Jonathan said. Then he casually continued eating his dinner.

The conviction with which this man spoke startled me. "Wait a minute," I said, "are you trying to tell me, if I start to find out what the mind *is* this will fix my problems?"

"That is exactly what I am saying," he replied.

"Analyzing and judging will get you nowhere. All you will find are the obvious games you play on yourself and others. One must go deeper, beyond the superficial games, beyond all the experiences related to the past, and SEE that it is one's own thought system that is responsible for carrying all illusionary negative feelings and behavioral patterns from the past."

I had taken courses in psychology for two years at the university and felt I was well enough informed to defeat my adversary on this point.

"Don't you believe in the Freudian theory that all our habits and behavioral patterns start in early child-hood?" I asked.

"Yes," Jonathan said, "I agree wholeheartedly that our behavioral patterns start then, however, there is more to that statement than meets the eye. You have to go deeper into the subconscious to realize that it was your own mind that picked up the habits and problems via an experience."

"I realize fully that we have to go deeper into the subconscious," I conceded. "I also agree that some doctrines are of little value and to hold on to the past is irrelevant. However, all my thoughts and behavioral patterns are a direct result of my experiences from the past and there is only so much I can do about that."

Looking at Jonathan, I had a feeling of smug con-tentment that I had finally trapped him into a corner.

"You're a fool," he stated.

"I beg your pardon," I blurted out, surprised at his words.

"I said you are a fool," he repeated. "Don't you see that you are still stuck in the past and have given up hope. It is theories like this that stop human beings from functioning in a stable manner and keep them in their dilemmas."

Second
Chance

All at once I felt deflated, and anger rose in me as I demanded: "How can you say that a traumatic experience from the past is illusionary when in fact it actually happened?"

"I'm afraid you have missed my point," Jonathan replied. "What I am saying is that the traumatic experience was real then, but *now* it is only an illusion from the past carried through time via thought."

"This is where most theories fail," he continued. "We blame parents, friends, events, and our memories of them instead of seeing that we are responsible for our own negative thought patterns. Most theories help convince the person that the mind is passive and incapable of freeing itself from the past." He paused. "Have you any idea how many people suffer needlessly because of this ridiculous theory? Have you any idea how many people are convinced that little hope exists for them in this reality?"

There was a long silence. "It appears you have read a substantial amount on this subject," I ventured.

"On the contrary," he replied, "I have read very little on the subject of the mind."

"If that is the case, how can you speak with such authority?" I questioned.

"Because I learned to SEE."

"That is a ridiculous statement," I said.

"Have it your way, believe as you wish, that is your prerogative in life. However, you are the one who has

20

the troubled mind and if you wish to relieve your anxieties, you will have to stop analyzing and trying to figure out the mysteries of life."

His statements were made in such a way that, though I did not understand, I felt just maybe, he was trying to convey something to me that was beyond my grasp.

"Listen, Richard, it doesn't matter to me if you SEE or not. On the other hand it would be nice if you found the help you seek."

My mind had never been in such turmoil. Once again this simple man had crushed my entire belief system with his unorthodox answers.

The waiter interrupted my thoughts as he asked if everything had been to our satisfaction. The bill was settled and we walked out into the warm evening air.

"It was a very interesting evening," Jonathan remarked. "I enjoyed both the dinner and our conversation."

I agreed that it had been one of the most unusual evenings of my life. "How would you like to spend some time by the pool at my hotel tomorrow?" I asked.

"Sorry, I can't, Richard. I am going to Hana tomorrow," he explained. "Why don't you come with me for the ride? I'll pick you up at your hotel at 9 A.M."

"Fine," I said. "See you tomorrow."

As I drove off, I was engrossed in thought. The eve-

Second
Chance

ning had left me totally confused yet Jonathan didn't expect me to figure it out. There were so many questions I wanted to ask.

# CHAPTER
# 3

I AWOKE the next morning after a restless night. Despite Jonathan's advice of "don't try to figure it out," my mind had gone over and over the things we had talked about.

After a shower and breakfast I walked towards the pool. As I approached I saw that Jonathan was already there.

"Good morning," I called.

"Morning," he replied. "Isn't this a lovely quiet spot?"

We stood there in silent admiration for a moment,

then Jonathan said, "I hope you enjoy the ride to Hana. The scenery is very picturesque."

"How far is it?" I asked. I was a little concerned in case my back gave me pain.

"It's about a three hour drive each way," he replied.

"That sounds fine." I had my pain pills with me and I really wanted to spend the day with this man.

Jonathan rose and said cheerfully, "Shall we be on our way?"

As we walked towards his car I told him how my mind had been churning all night.

He smiled. "The trouble is you are trying to figure it all out. If you try to figure it out, all you can possibly see is your present acquired thought patterns and ideas."

"I really have no other choice," I responded.

Jonathan, ignoring my statement, said, "Why don't we forget all about your problems and enjoy the beauty of Maui?"

Soon we were on our journey and I found myself captivated by the beauty around me. I was fascinated by the many faces of Maui.

First we drove through miles of sugar cane, then further on we were in the midst of pineapple plantations. Here and there were incredible vistas of the ocean where thunderous waves crashed against the shoreline.

As we continued on our way the scenery changed to

rolling meadows. As far as the eye could see there were cattle grazing peacefully in the morning sun. We stopped for a while to admire the skill of both the cowboys and the horses. I had not seen this before, and I found it extremely entertaining to watch the Hawaiian cowboys round up the inevitable stray.

We continued our journey to Hana and once again Maui changed her face; this time to one of mountainous, tropical terrain. The road narrowed as it wound its way along the mountainside.

The drive was peaceful and the everchanging scenery interested me until I started to think again. I had so many questions—questions I really wanted answers to. For instance, what did Jonathan mean when he said, "a traumatic experience from the past may have been real *then* but *now* it is only an illusion carried through time via thought."

And another thing: why was he so against going into the past to fix any emotional problems?

Finally I asked him outright why he thought this way. He gave me a quick glance.

"The further into the past you go, the more details you remember and therefore, the more complications you put in the way of the solution."

I confronted him with the fact that I thought the details of a traumatic experience were very important.

"They are if you wish to keep them alive," he replied. "The details," he continued, "are simply proof

*Second Chance*

to the ego that the problem exists. They perpetuate the situation you are trying to get rid of.

"Going back into the negative past to find happiness is like trying to make a silk purse out of a sow's ear," he added.

"Are you saying all doctrines that go into the past are wrong?" I asked.

"No, I am not saying anything is *wrong*, I am simply saying it's a matter of evolution.

"As mankind evolves in consciousness, these theories are outgrown. They become merely pointless states with no true conscious recognition. Here is where it is necessary to go beyond theories to a clearer state of SEEING."

Once again Jonathan was using that darned word SEEING. The word bothered me. I still had no idea what he meant by SEEING.

"Can you tell me what you really mean by SEEING?" I pleaded.

"No, I'm sorry I can't! SEEING is a state which must be experienced."

"Surely you can at least give me a clue."

With a huge grin on his face he said, "Okay. I'll try, but remember that the words I use are trying to describe the indescribable.

"SEEING is what evolves man's mind to a higher level of consciousness. It is this evolvement that enables him to psychologically understand himself and the world around him."

"Do you honestly expect people to believe what you are saying?"

"No, I don't expect people to believe what I am saying but I am not trying to tell 'people'. I am simply telling *you* my philosophical point of view."

The way he said it touched me deeply. I felt I had truly found someone who cared.

We travelled in silence for a time and then turned off the main road onto a gravel driveway, at the end of which was a well groomed yard and a cottage-style house. As we approached, the door burst open and three excited little children ran out, followed by a lovely young Hawaiian lady. The car had barely stopped before we were besieged by the three children shouting "Uncle Jonathan."

The two older children jumped into Jonathan's arms and hugged him but the smallest one froze when she saw me and took two steps backwards to be close to her mother. Picking up the small child, the mother embraced Jonathan with a fond "Aloha."

Jonathan introduced me to the young lady, whose name was Lana, and to her three children: Jim aged 9, Ana aged 7, and last but not least, little Rosa who was celebrating her third birthday. This was the reason for all the excitement.

Jonathan opened the trunk of the car and brought out a huge birthday parcel gaily wrapped. We all laughed as the excitement of the present was almost too much for the little one. Later two more parcels were discovered, one for each of the other children.

It was a hot day but the mountain breeze kept a certain freshness in the air. The children, enthused with their presents, ran off to play and Lana set a table laden with fresh tropical fruits and salads. As we ate, Lana talked about her husband, Toma, who was a carpenter by trade.

It was obvious that Toma and Lana were proud of their family and home. Everything was clean and well cared for. Lana appeared to be someone who really loved her family and was completely content with life.

We sat on the lawn under a palm tree and talked about various subjects. I was extremely impressed by Lana's intelligence. Her philosophy of life was one of positivity. It was apparent that she was not only beautiful in appearance but also in nature.

After a relaxing two hour visit we said goodbye to everyone and headed for home. The day had been a wonderful holiday, full of gratifying experiences.

# CHAPTER
## 4

JONATHAN had given me a lot of "food for thought." Since our trip to Hana, the last few days had been full and very enjoyable for me. It was, in fact, a very long time since I had felt such enthusiasm for life. It was like a breath of fresh air and I felt very grateful for it.

There were still many things he'd said that didn't make sense, and before leaving Maui I wanted to clarify them. I found myself reaching for his telephone number and as I walked towards the phone I started to think how unusual a person Jonathan really was. He appeared as an intelligent, well dressed professional man, not unlike many I knew, but the way he thought and talked was completely different. His voice on the other end of the line interrupted my thoughts and we made arrangements to meet that same afternoon.

When Jonathan arrived the sun was hot, so we decided to sit by the pool. When we were settled in our deck chairs I thanked him for the pleasant day he had shared with me on our trip to Hana and said, "There is something I would like to ask you, Jonathan. My professor believed psychology was a true science yet others say it is not. What do you think?"

"Psychology is a science, of course it is. It is as much a science as physics or whatever, because it is created from a constant basic factor. There is a common denominator."

"What is that?" I asked.

"*Mind*," he replied. "From mind all psychological behavior is born, all concepts, rituals and dogmas. All mental functions are mind created.

"There is also a second common denominator and that is thought, so we have two common denominators. One is mind and the other is thought. By definition, psychology is the science of mind and from these two principles true psychology is born."

Listening to his answer confirmed my suspicion that Jonathan spoke with a greater depth of understanding than one would ordinarily expect. Little did I know at this time, what a profound effect my encounter with this man was going to have on my life.

After a few moments of silence I asked Jonathan what he did for a living.

"I retired a few years ago. Before that I worked for thirty years at various jobs."

"You must take good physical care of yourself," I said. "You certainly don't look like someone who has worked for so many years. Another thing that fascinates me is that you are so calm and understanding. Have you always been this way?"

"Heavens no!" he replied. "Most of my life was pure hell. I walked through life as a very insecure person full of inhibitions. My life was mundane and full of sickness.

"It wasn't until I learned to SEE, that my life began to take some order. It was then I realized that my past was the *disorder* and by dropping my disorderly thoughts and feelings my life changed to one of order. I learned to free myself from my *own* negative thought patterns.

"Now, when I look back into the past I SEE it without disorder, knowing there was a reason for everything that happened to me."

There was a long pause, then Jonathan broke into a long smile.

"Don't take everything so seriously," he said. "Give yourself time to enjoy life."

His unusual answers bewildered me. "Do you realize that sometimes you are very difficult to understand?" I ventured.

Jonathan chuckled at my statement.

"Do you know other people who can SEE?" I
asked. "Are there any here on Maui?"

"There are people all over the world who SEE. You
may meet them but your own preconceived ideas may
stop you from recognizing their knowledge."

We sat quietly for a few moments. I really didn't
know what to say. Then Jonathan said, "There is a spe-
cial friend of mine who lives on the Island of Kauai.
She is without a doubt the most powerful person I
have ever met. She lives in a separate reality from
most people. Her knowledge of life and its workings is
unbelievable. She is one of the few people I know who
has found the power to go beyond SEEING into the
world of KNOWING."

I was about to ask what KNOWING meant, when
Jonathan, as if he could read my mind, said, "Don't
ask me what KNOWING means because that definitely cannot be explained."

"Does your friend talk to many people?" I inquired.

"No, she sees very few people. She enjoys her
privacy."

"I'd really like to talk to someone like that," I suggested. "It would be most interesting."

Jonathan's eyes twinkled and he chuckled to

himself.

"What are you smiling at?" I asked.

"Oh, I'm just imagining you and my friend encountering each other. It would be a very interesting situation, an unforgettable one, I assure you."

He was quiet for a moment and then he said, "You know, Richard, a long time ago she prophesied that in the eighties on the American continent there would appear a new psychology and psychiatry that would change the course of history. This movement would bring about miraculous healings beyond the imagination of modern day psychology."

I couldn't believe my ears and in total disbelief I said, "What an extraordinary statement to make. Did she say how all this would come about?"

"Yes! She said that a *few* doctors would start to realize to a deeper degree the secret of MIND and that this would revolutionize the whole science of psychology."

"Do you believe that this will happen?" I asked.

"Yes! I do," he replied.

Shaking my head, I thought Jonathan's story astounding and now I was even more intrigued at the prospect of meeting his friend.

"What does it take to see this lady?" I asked.

"There are some things you will have to learn first," Jonathan replied.

"What kind of things?" I persisted.

"First you must learn to listen and this will take courage."

"Why should it take courage to listen to someone's point of view?"

"Please, get it out of your head that what she says is a point of view. It is a *fact*."

"Don't you think I am a good listener?" I queried.

"Before I answer that question let me ask you two things. Do you or don't you wish to find some peace in your life? If so, are you willing to look and have the courage to listen?"

"Yes, I would love to find some answers to help me live what is left of my life."

Jonathan looked at me closely for a moment and then went on. "You asked why courage was needed to listen. When you encounter *true knowledge* it uncovers the empirical principles you now live by and forces you to look at life anew. This disturbs your ego which is your own worst enemy."

"When your ego is attacked it fights back with fear. This fear creates your insecurity, hate, desire, jealousy and all your negative behavioral patterns. As a matter of fact, it governs your whole life."

"I hear what you are saying," I said, "and I agree to a point that many people don't listen during a conversation. However, I feel personally that I am a good listener. As a matter of fact, all my life I have prided myself on my ability to listen and memorize."

Jonathan said nothing and bowed his head as if accepting my statement.

"First of all I must point out that you have HEARD nothing and SEEN nothing of what I have told you in the past few days. That prize ego of yours has trapped you in an existence and won't let you break the limitations you have put on yourself. If you wish to SEE, you will have to learn to accept a fact when you hear one. Don't listen to the words. *Listen* for a feeling."

"How can I possibly listen for a feeling?"

"Stop asking silly questions and *listen*. It is *listening* that allows you to receive the *feeling*. It is the feeling that has the power, not the knowledge. Knowledge without a feeling is simply memorized words, and is of very little value. Positive feelings make words come alive and allow you to SEE your neuroses and behavioral patterns for what they are."

"I don't understand that. Most theories agree that the ego is of value, and now you are saying that it is detrimental. Is not the ego important for our self-esteem?"

"As far as self-esteem is concerned, it is the ego that destroys it. Self-esteem is a state of contentment and well being. When the ego is on top of the pile it has the illusionary qualities of self-esteem, however, as soon as the ego is challenged or jarred from its position, instead of self-esteem, it creates fear, jealousy, desire, anger, hate and insecurity. These are the perfect ingredients for a very unhappy person living an unstable life."

I wanted to challenge him on his statement but before I could speak he said, "*Listen*. A conversation is interesting and can be quite informative. A debate on the other hand is two or more people expounding different points of view with their egos trying to prove that they are right.

"When this happens there is an extraordinary effect on people. Instead of listening to each other and sharing their philosophical ideas, inevitably the ego attacks its adversary's position by condemning all statements that are contrary to its own way of thinking. The conversation is then nothing but a word game; the whole philosophical conversation is turned into verbal piffle.

"Some people also believe that arguing stimulates their thinking faculties but if you take a closer look you will see it has an adverse effect. It creates a mental barrier with each person only interested in finding an opening to discredit their adversary. Such people therefore go through life with an inverted outlook, never learning anything new."

"I still don't understand, Jonathan. Why should someone be afraid to listen?"

"That is twice today you have asked the same question and the answer is still the same."

Bewildered by Jonathan's reply I felt the better part

Second
Chance

of valour was to keep quiet and forget any further *debate*.

We sat watching the guests enjoying themselves in the cool, turquoise pool under the blazing Maui sun. As late afternoon approached we agreed to meet for supper at a later date.

# CHAPTER 5

W HAT Jonathan said about ego was definitely different from what I had been taught in class. I wondered what my old professor would think of Jonathan's theories and concepts. I was intrigued because if Jonathan's statement that ego is detrimental to one's mental stability was true, most of my psychological training was invalidated.

The next time I saw Jonathan I decided to ask him but before I could question him on the subject he asked me if I had a good doctor.

"Yes, I have a terrific fellow who is very conscientious. He is more than just my doctor; he has been my personal friend for years."

"That's nice to hear. You know a lot can happen in two years. There are many clever doctors and one of these days, one of them will come up with a cure."

I elaborated and expressed the various ideas some well-known doctors had come out with lately, and how the medical authorities were trying everything possible to stamp out cancer.

Speaking of my problem quickly brought to mind the true reality of my existing illness, and I felt grateful for meeting Jonathan. He had helped me get over the feelings of loneliness and fear that haunted me when I first arrived in Maui.

Pulling myself from my reminiscence I realized that I had been in Maui for eight days and had not yet seen a Hawaiian show. I asked Jonathan if he knew of one.

"As a matter of fact, there is a tremendous show at the Maui Lu tonight. It's a very nice place to dine as well."

Soon I was on the phone and the reservations were confirmed. The rest of the evening was pleasant as we dined and were entertained Hawaiian style. Jonathan was in good spirits as the entertainers chose people from the audience to join in the hula dance. When the show finished we walked outside and sat under a palm tree. The evening was warmer than it had been earlier. It really gave me the sensation of being in the tropics.

Turning to Jonathan, I queried him once again. "What you said about ego fascinates me, but I just can't follow your reasoning when you say that the ego is detrimental to our mental stability. It bothers me. My ego is important to me and there is no way I would like to lose it."

"Have you ever heard me say you can *lose* your ego? That, my dear Richard, is impossible. You can only find out what ego *is* so that it will have less control over you. Then you will stop having to prove yourself to the world and the *feeling* of contentment and self-esteem will be yours."

When he said that, a memory from my past was triggered. One particular awareness group I had attended came to mind and I started to tell Jonathan how we were told to prove ourselves by not going to the bathroom for twenty-four hours. I related to Jonathan how embarrassed I felt at the ridiculous situation I had placed myself in. "The therapist kept telling me to prove to myself that I could do it."

Laughing uproariously, Jonathan said he thought that was one of the funniest things he had ever heard in his life. Even to me, the whole scene and my part in it appeared totally bizarre.

After his hilarity subsided, Jonathan asked me if it had helped me at all. "I thought so at the time," I answered, "but now I see it was just a crazy exercise with a placebo effect." At this Jonathan broke into peals of laughter again.

"What else have you done to prove this prize ego of yours?"

"Oh, yes! I was once told by a therapist to be up-front with everyone and tell people how I really felt. That same evening I told someone all the weak points of his character."

"What happened?" inquired Jonathan.

"He threatened me violently."

This answer made Jonathan stand up, roaring with laughter, and hold his chest as if he were in pain. "Hell, you're a funny man," he gasped. By this time both of us were laughing so much we ached.

In a little while we calmed down. Breaking the silence, I said, "Tell me, Jonathan, where did you learn all these theories of yours?"

"Remember, I told you about my friend that lives on Kauai. Well, one day I HEARD her and that was the day I learned to SEE."

"What did you HEAR?" I queried.

"I HEARD her say that it was my *own* thought system that created its own insecurity. After that, as if by magic, I could SEE and HEAR people playing their roles in life. I SAW my own role as an act, just like everyone else's. Part of my role was to feel insecure.

"I SAW the world as a perfect state, and realized that we truly are the actors in this big illusion called life. I SAW that the whole world is connected to what man calls *mind*.

"From here I started to SEE with clarity that it was my own thought pattern that created my behavioral pattern. It became so apparent to me that when my thought patterns were negative, so was my behavior. Then it was simple to see that if I had a negative thought from the past, I reacted negatively *now*! It was simple logic that if my past was full of negative feelings it would be psychological suicide to wander back into it.

"This is where most psychological and awareness groups fail. They blame the past for the person's own weakness. All my life I blamed either my mother or my father or my upbringing or my schooling for my faults. Always something else was stopping me from being happy. Do you know what kept me so unhappy? My ego!

"That same lady told me that the little mind and the ego are one and the same. I couldn't understand her at all. However, when I SAW it was ego that was causing my psychological problems, the riddle of ego and mind being one made more sense to me."

I had to admit that I didn't really understand the meaning of Jonathan's statement that ego and the little mind are the same thing. To me it was very perplexing and certainly just his opinion. I confessed to Jonathan that I was still bewildered and confused about ego.

"It is ego that forces you to prove yourself," he explained, "and in so doing creates the feeling of insecurity. It is ego that creates wars and allows starvation throughout the world. It is ego that is responsible for jealousy, hate, anger and greed. It is ego that takes all your negative memories from the past and uses them against you. It is ego that creates all psychological confusion."

I honestly couldn't comprehend his explanation. I only knew I felt confused as my mind tried to ascertain what Jonathan was saying.

Before the evening was over I wanted Jonathan to answer one more question. "What about the components of the personality such as Freud's id, ego, and super-ego? Where do they fit into your theory?"

Appearing somewhat surprised at my question, he shook his head from side to side and accused me of asking the darndest questions.

"The ego," he responded, "is your personalized idea of who and what you are. Ego is an image of self-importance. This image of yourself is brought about by a thought system with the power of *mind* behind it, to bring your thoughts into the reality you now see.

"Don't you see, all these components of the personality are made from illusionary thoughts? In short: id, ego, and super-ego are all made from the ignorance of the little mind. They have no substance of their own other than that which the personalized self allows. If you keep insisting on their existence, all you will have is a lot of extremely well defined illusions."

At this point Jonathan looked at me and chuckled. "Don't try to figure it out. You will only waste your time. *Listen* for a *feeling*."

His smile broadened as he asked, "I wonder why he threatened you?" With this he burst into laughter, said he had to leave and assured me that he had enjoyed the whole evening.

"Laughter is a wonderful remedy," he concluded. We shook hands and parted.

# CHAPTER
# 6

**T**WO days later I met Jonathan in Lahaina. We met in the same spot we had the first time. For me it was one of those days when everything seemed to go wrong. My back had ached all night, I had a headache and even Hawaii looked dismal to me. The beauty I had seen the first night I arrived was no longer there. We sat on the stone wall and I turned to Jonathan and asked him again about the phenomenon of SEEING and HEARING. I suggested the reason we differed on the subject was one of semantics and that was why communication was lost during our conversations.

*Second Chance*

He assured me that was not the case. He said if I wanted to learn to SEE and HEAR I would have to stop tying to figure it out and forget about semantics.

"It's like this, Richard: seeing and hearing are memorized processes from the little mind. They enable us to relate known data to each other via our intellect.

"On the other hand SEEING and HEARING are not physical processes; rather, they lie outside the known realm of the so-called little mind. When this phenomenon takes place it raises your level of consciousness which starts to bring some new understanding of your own psychological manifestations. It reveals the connection of mind to your behavioral patterns. It gives you a second chance in life. It lets you SEE beyond your preconceived ideas of life. SEEING starts to show you the fallacy of going into the past to fix your psychological problems."

"I hear what you are saying, Jonathan, and I appreciate your way of thinking. However, there are many theories on the mind and how it works. I personally go along with the belief that the mind is the anatomy and physiology of the brain and nothing more."

"That's quite a mouthful," Jonathan said as if he were impressed. "However," he went on, "it's a bunch of utter rubbish. If you keep thinking in this manner you will see only your own preconceived ideas of life and find nothing new. It is such thoughts that set limitations on yourself. You have to separate mind from thought because they are two different things. They take different roles in life."

"If mind is neither a thing, nor a thought, what is it?" I asked.

"It is a psychic power which acts as a catalyst and turns your thoughts, whether conscious or unconscious, into the reality you now see."

Jonathan had expressed quite a few unusual theories but I felt none so outlandish as the statement that the mind is a source of power separate from our thought system. I related my feelings about this matter and mentioned the incredulous thoughts my old professor would have had if anyone in his class had suggested such an absurd theory. I assured him that his concept would not be accepted and again I challenged him by asking, "If mind is a separate source from thought, what is thought?"

"Thought is nothing more than a vehicle to assist you to play the game of life." He elaborated on his statement by saying, "Thought has no power of its own. Thought is but a conveyor and the power of MIND creates the manifestation of the thought."

He went on to explain that when his thought system believed he was insecure, that is exactly how he felt and behaved in life. "When I realized this for a fact," Jonathan continued, "my insecurity and all related behavioral patterns started to change to security,

49

bringing some stability and order to my life."

I was always somewhat amazed at the ease with which Jonathan answered my questions, yet I couldn't help thinking, "It can't be that simple."

When I expressed my views on this point he simply shrugged his shoulders. His nonchalant attitude gave me twinges of anger, especially when he refused to defend his statements. It was an exasperating predicament. Most people I knew would defend their point of view. He looked at me and smiled. That bothered me because I didn't know why he was amused by my statement.

Then he said, "That same old lady I told you about earlier once said to me, 'An intellectual person is one who can integrate and discuss various theories and concepts. A wise person is one who ignores them completely!'"

This statement surprised me, and I didn't know quite what to say except that I thought it was a 'closed mind' situation when someone refused to *debate*.

Jonathan looked at me with a twinkle in his eye. "What's wrong?" he said, "Did you get out of bed on the wrong side this morning?"

"A lot of things are bothering me. My back and my head ache. To be truthful, I feel awful. I feel full of anger towards life."

"Ah, forget it," Jonathan said. "We all have days like that."

*Second Chance*

He told me he was leaving Maui the following day to visit friends on Kauai. It jarred me to realize that this would perhaps be our last day together. I expressed my feelings about meeting him and told him how much he had added to my holiday and that I found his philosophical theories extremely interesting, though I didn't understand or believe a lot of them.

"Why don't you come to my house," Jonathan asked, "and have a rest if you feel tired? It's only a couple of miles down the road."

Thanking him, I declined. I thought it better to go back to my hotel and rest. We shook hands and parted, agreeing to meet for dinner at the Pioneer Inn.

As I started the car, thoughts were racing through my head. Jonathan had spoken of different levels of consciousness. I had explained to him that many people take offense at statements about higher and lower levels. He had looked at me in disbelief and instead of answering my question, asked me why I had gone to consciousness raising groups and why had I taken psychology courses at university?

"To get a better understanding of myself," I had replied.

"Therefore," Jonathan said, "you were trying to get a deeper understanding of how your mind works, right?"

I agreed. He looked at me intently for a moment

then said, "Deeper understanding can only come
when there is some movement in your level of consciousness. Listen," he said in an abrupt manner,
"why don't you take that prize ego of yours out of the
way and *listen* to what *you* are saying.

"First you tell me that you went to consciousness
raising awareness groups, then you tell me that you
don't believe in different levels of consciousness. Are
you honestly trying to tell me that the great mystics
and wise men of the past were on the same level of
consciousness as you or I?"

Jonathan pulled no punches. The astuteness of his
statement fascinated me and at the same time, disturbed me. I had the feeling he had participated in
many awareness groups so I asked him if this were the
case?

"No, I have never participated in any such activity," he replied. "I am not a joiner of groups or organi-
zations. It's not that I have anything against them; it is
simply my choice."

He ended the conversation by asking, "Wouldn't it
be a boring life if there weren't greater levels of consciousness for us to find?"

# CHAPTER 7

LATER that evening I entered the courtyard of the Pioneer Inn and saw Jonathan seated at a table.

"Good evening, Richard."

"Good evening," I replied. I sat down and almost immediately the waiter was at the table taking our order. When he left I said, "I never thought of coming to Hawaii for a holiday before. It never held any interest for me. Now I wish I had come years ago."

"It sounds like you are enjoying Maui," Jonathan said.

"Yes, I am."

*Second Chance*

Jonathan listened attentively as I told him about my life as an executive. The twelve-hour working day with all the job-related pressures and decisions that go along with the position. At times my head felt like it was going to burst.

One day someone suggested that meditation would help alleviate some of my tensions and anxieties. Everything seemed to work for a short while, but then I got to the point where I found it frustrating to stick to my routine of meditating. It wasn't always convenient or I just didn't feel like doing my exercise, yet it bothered me if I skipped the time I had allotted.

"It's like you're damned if you do and you're damned if you don't." With this we both smiled at the double bind.

"Do you believe in meditation?" I asked, "and do you meditate?"

"Yes, I think meditation is a beautiful way to help relax an overactive mind. As for your second question, yes, I do meditate, but I don't do it as a timed ritual!"

"If you don't stick to a routine, what do you do?"

"Sometimes I look at the beauty of the ocean. Sometimes I take a quiet walk or I simply sit in my armchair. There is no fixed way to get oneself into the *state* of meditation. The *state* of meditation comes when the ego is put to sleep 'via silence'.

"The ego mind, sometimes called the little mind, depends on activity. When this activity gets out of

control, the possibility of a nervous breakdown becomes a reality."

"Meditation is a silent mind. It is silence that clears
the psychic channels and enables you to see life with
more clarity. This clarity in turn will bring the answers to relieve your anxieties and frustrations, thus
giving you a more stable and orderly life."

I was impressed by Jonathan's theory of meditation,
but I told him I was taught, and still felt, that determi-
nation to stick to an orderly and timed routine for
meditating was important.

"Didn't you just tell me that the *ritual* of meditating
created a form of stress for you and added to the stress-
ful nature of your situation?"

I conceded that might be true in my case because I
wasn't willing to persevere. For those who have the
incentive to succeed, the little stress created seemed
hardly mentionable.

"Richard, listen to me! Stress is stress! All stress is
dangerous to a stable mind and our being as a whole.
It is stress that creates a lot of our mental and physical
problems. It is stress that leads to an unbalanced
mind, which can lead to alcoholism, drug addiction,
divorce, management and employee disturbances.
Stress is a form of mental anguish that leads to mental
breakdowns—anger and violence usually being the
end product."

The waiter arrived with our dinner. While we ate I

asked Jonathan to tell me about Kauai.

"It's called the Garden Isle," he said, "and it has a different beauty from Maui. It's very lush but I really can't describe it to you. One must experience the island."

Earlier Jonathan had mentioned the name of a very wise lady who lived on Kauai so I asked him to tell me more about this intriguing person.

Jonathan smiled as he said, "It is difficult to describe her. She is quite different from most people.

"You know, Richard, it's a strange thing, you remind me so much of myself a long time ago. Like you, I lost my wife and came for a holiday hoping to get some rest. The ordeal of losing my wife had exhausted me physically and mentally so I came to Kauai planning a two week vacation. The first week I stayed in a hotel where the majority of guests were tourists from the mainland. One morning I felt the need for something different so I packed my suitcases and took a ride in the most dilapidated old bus I had ever seen.

"It was quite an adventure as the old bus made its way along narrow winding roads. After an hour's hair-raising journey, the bus finally stopped and everyone scrambled off leaving me sitting alone. The bus driver suggested that I could stay at the nearby village of Hanapepe.

"A couple of evenings later I was strolling along the beach, wondering what life was all about and why my wife had to die at such an early age, when I heard an "Aloha." I looked around and there was a beautiful old Hawaiian lady who spoke in a very gentle, soft voice. We talked about the beauty of the evening sky and she introduced herself as Lila. We talked for nearly two hours.

"When I first listened to her I thought she was a bit crazy, the way she spoke of hidden powers that were available at will.

"I listened in fascination as she spoke about separate realities. Most of the time I didn't understand her at all, yet I felt she was trying to tell me something. Unfortunately my own fear stopped me from HEARING. As a matter of fact my fear was so strong, I ran from that village with my tail between my legs, so to speak.

"It wasn't until one day, nearly two years later, for no apparent reason, that I started to think about my unusual encounter with the old lady. The more I thought about her the more I felt compelled to revisit Lila and face whatever made me feel so insecure in her presence."

I listened intently while Jonathan told his story. Finally, I asked him what it was she had said that scared him so much.

"That is really a difficult question to answer," he said. "All I can tell you is that she spoke in such an unusual way that I couldn't understand her. What little I did grasp, was so foreign that it psychologically troubled me."

"What did she talk about that fascinated you?"

"She spoke of hidden powers beyond man's mental comprehension."

As Jonathan spoke of his adventure, a serenity spread over his face. "Perhaps I am boring you with my escapades," he suggested.

"On the contrary," I replied. "I am enjoying hearing of your adventures on Kauai."

Suddenly, the thought occurred to me that I had enough time left to visit Kauai and see the island for myself. I asked Jonathan the name of a good hotel and he suggested the Coco Palms.

"Great," I said. "Who knows, I may see you over there."

Second
Chance

# CHAPTER 8

THREE days later I flew to the island of Kauai on Aloha Airways. It was a pleasant forty-five minute flight. On my arrival I was met by a courtesy bus which took me to the Coco Palms Hotel. I was told that at one time this place had been a coconut plantation. The owners of the hotel had managed to capture some of the past in the decor and landscaping, giving guests a feeling of old Hawaii.

After I had settled in my room, I took a stroll through the grounds. A feeling of excitement was with me at the thought of my new adventure in Kauai.

# Second Chance

Kauai was quieter than Maui and it definitely had more vegetation and color. I could see why it was called the Garden Isle. I felt it was an ideal spot to rest and unwind for the remainder of my holiday.

Two days passed and I had not seen or heard from Jonathan. On the evening of the third day I was walking through the well manicured grounds, and to my surprise Jonathan appeared and greeted me with a big smile.

"It's really nice to see you again," I said, shaking his hand. We talked about the islands and our adventures since we had last seen each other. It was a pleasant kind of evening as the trade winds swept across the island bringing relief from the afternoon's scorching sun.

To my delight, Jonathan invited me to a luau that some of his friends were giving that evening and soon we were in my car going towards a beach near Kilauea Bay. After a short journey, we arrived at a beautiful little cove with fine white sand, surrounded by palm trees and lush vegetation. The sand displayed an ever changing array of colors as the sun made its descent for another day.

There were about thirty people gathered on the beach. A group of them started to strum guitars and soon the beach was full of soft Hawaiian music accompanied by lilting voices. Jonathan introduced me to the rest of the guests, and by now the aroma drifting from the imu was a gastronomic delight.

The music stopped and out of the surrounding bush walked two women and a man. Jonathan went over to greet them. He introduced them as Mr. and Mrs. Makua, parents of Lana whom I had met in Hana. With them was a most beautiful lady. A lady with charisma, such as I had never felt from any other human being. He introduced her as Mamma Lila.

She spoke in a very soft, gentle voice with a strong Hawaiian accent. This petite and dignified lady was escorted to a seat reserved for her. When she was seated, the air once again filled with music as the Hawaiian guitarists played and sang.

An announcement that the food was ready brought cries of delight from everyone, especially the younger children. After we had eaten I asked Jonathan to tell me more about Mamma Lila.

He stood up and said, "Let's stretch our legs." We walked along the beach and he told me that Mamma Lila, as she is known to her friends, is a unique lady. "There are many rumors about her. Some see her as a rather fascinating philosopher, others see her as a mystic, and some see her as just plain crazy. It is said she has the gift of 'ike-pápálua.'"

"The gift of what?" I asked.

Jonathan smiled, "The gift of 'ike-pápálua means 'one who can see double', or 'the gift of second sight'."

I asked him to explain exactly what he meant by

seeing double or the gift of second sight.

"That is beyond my knowledge to explain," he said. "Perhaps Mamma Lila will explain it to you if you ask her."

"It doesn't really matter," I replied offhandedly. "I was just curious."

With this Jonathan slapped me on the back and we headed back to the luau. When we arrived I looked around at the scene before my eyes, swaying palm trees, Hawaiian guitar music, melodious voices singing and children romping in the moonlit water. I had to pinch myself to see if I was dreaming. I wondered what my associates in New York would say if they were here.

The whole evening was a foreign experience to me and the thought of talking to Mamma Lila made me feel tremendously insecure since Jonathan had told me she had the power of second sight. I assumed that to mean she could read my thoughts and I asked Jonathan if this were possible.

"That's an old wive's tale," he chuckled. "No one can read your mind. Mind is the most private thing there is. Come with me and we will say good night to Mamma Lila."

As we approached I could see that she was preparing to depart. She looked up at me and smiled. "How are you enjoying your vacation in Kauai?"

Instead of simply answering her question, I started

to relate some of my experiences since meeting Jonathan in Maui, mentioning some of his rather outlandish theories. I quoted clichés I had memorized from my limited psychological training and at the same time I expressed my strong desire to understand more of the mysteries of life.

In a gentle but firm manner she said, "Pursuing true knowledge takes more than just mental desire."

Turning to Jonathan, Mamma Lila suggested that he bring me to her home the following evening around five. With this she said good-night to everyone and departed.

After she had gone, Jonathan remarked that I was a very lucky person. He told me that few people have the honor of being invited to her home. He went on to say that when he had first met Mamma Lila, he couldn't figure her out and at first he thought perhaps it was a cultural difference.

"However," he said, "it didn't take long to realize that this was not the case."

The way Jonathan spoke of his experiences with Mamma Lila fascinated me and I asked him to give me an example of what he really meant. He scratched his head and considered for a moment, then he said, "Remember when I told you Mamma Lila and I met on the beach and that she scared the living daylights out of me? What I didn't tell you, was that she knew more about me than I knew about myself."

"That's impossible," I declared.

"Is it?" Jonathan asked in a very casual way.

What Jonathan had said about Mamma Lila intrigued me but at the same time I must admit that I was full of disbelief. However, curiosity got the better of me and I asked Jonathan if he could explain such a phenomenon.

"I'm afraid not. All I can tell you is that Mamma Lila is a very extraordinary lady."

As Jonathan talked about Mamma Lila, a feeling of excitement rose in me at the thought of actually meeting such a person. Always the preconceived fantasy of the event was far, far removed from the actual reality.

It was amazing how quickly Jonathan spotted my dilemma. Putting an arm around my shoulders, he said, "By the expression on your face you look as though you would qualify as a fully paid up member of the I.C.B.—the Institute for the Chronically Bewildered, but don't worry, you are not alone. It has the biggest membership of all institutes."

With this statement we both had a good laugh and made the necessary arrangements to meet Mamma Lila the following evening.

# CHAPTER 9

THE Coco Palms in the early morning was a beautiful sight to me after living in New York. I wanted to spend as much time in the sun as possible during my vacation, so I dressed and took my morning stroll through the beautiful grounds.

I couldn't help thinking of my unusual encounter with two people such as Jonathan and Mamma Lila. The way they viewed life was highly irregular to say the least. Regardless of this, they were both interesting and unusual conversationalists who had added greatly to my Hawaiian vacation.

Second
Chance

As late afternoon approached I looked forward to having an evening with Mamma Lila. Jonathan arrived on schedule and soon we were on our way. Neither Jonathan nor I said much to each other as we drove.

My reverie was interrupted when Jonathan swung into a narrow driveway which led to a clearing that displayed a little house built of coral. As we approached, Mamma Lila appeared with open arms and graciously welcomed us to her home.

The interior was decorated in a simple but comfortable style. The cleanliness of it impressed me. The whole house seemed to shine.

Mamma Lila was in the process of cooking dinner. The aroma plus the warm surroundings recalled childhood memories of visiting my grandmother when I was a young boy.

Jonathan and I were ushered onto a patio overlooking a small bay with white sand and gently swaying palms. The water was almost still as the sunset once again showed its many colors. There was a serenity about the scene in front of me that was indescribable.

After a few minutes Mamma Lila announced that dinner was served. We ate in silence for a while, then I asked Mamma Lila, "Have you always lived here on the island of Kauai?"

"No," she replied, "in my lifetime I have lived on most of the islands at one time or another. I spent my childhood on the island of Lanai where my parents worked in the hala kahiki fields. It was also there that I met and married my late husband. Then as a young couple, we left Lanai and went to live on Maui where we had our two children. Several years later we moved here to Kauai."

The topic of conversation then turned towards the history of some of the islands. It impressed me to hear how much Jonathan knew about the Hawaiian culture. His respect for the Hawaiian Islands and the people was clearly sincere.

By this time we had finished dinner and Mamma Lila stood up and asked me if I would escort her down a reddish earth path which led to the beach. We sat on a little grass knoll, watching the deep colors of the late sunset change from minute to minute.

Inadvertently my thoughts went back to "Why me? Why can't I live to be the same age as Mamma Lila?" I looked up from my dismal thoughts and saw that Mamma Lila and Jonathan were looking out to sea with a serenity that I had never seen before. A feeling of sheer loneliness swept over me, my chest swelled and tears ran down my cheeks. I thought I had left this unbearable feeling in New York but here it was in Kauai.

Mamma Lila sensed my emotional turmoil and turning, she grasped both my hands and asked, "Is there anything you would like to talk about?"

*Second Chance*

With a feeling of relief I started to relate the same story I had told Jonathan the first night we had met. There was a long silence while Mamma Lila sat in contemplation, then she asked, "Do you fear death?"

"Yes," I answered. "The thought of it gives me many sleepless nights."

"Death is nothing to fear," she replied. "Beyond life lies beauty. Beyond life lies peace and tranquility. At death, this world you now know stops and the full illumination of *Mind* is born. This shows you your innocence of life and allows you to see the true beauty of yourself."

It was an incredible statement and for some unknown reason helped to alleviate the anxiety I was undergoing. We sat looking at the view which by this time was breathtaking.

Mamma Lila remarked how lucky we were to witness such beauty, then turning to Jonathan she said, "The evening is full of Mana. It is a perfect time to capture spirit power."

Mana was an unfamiliar word to me, so I asked her what she meant by it.

"Mana, my young friend, is a power that holds the secret to your very existence. Mana on its own has neither definite shape nor form, yet it is in everything that exists.

"Mana is the power that holds this world of ours together. Mana is pure energy. It is virtually impossible for anyone to explain what Mana really is because it is of spirit essence. Mana cannot be seen by the naked eye. It must be absorbed by a *positive feeling*.

"It is Mana that helps wash away the illusionary values you place on life. It is the sustenance of the wise."

I assured her that I did not base my life on illusionary values but rather on very realistic ones.

She answered by saying, "Be careful. 'Realistic' can be very deceiving."

"What do you mean by that?" I inquired.

"All life is brought about by mankind's own doing. This world you now see is a figment of your own imagination."

Again my mind tried to evaluate the credibility of such statements. "Surely you can't say these palm trees, the sky, and the ocean are not real!" I said.

With the movements of a graceful dancer, Mamma Lila gestured with her hands while explaining her statements. "This reality you now see is but a reflection of thought," she said. "There are many realities, young man, but the ideal reality is a world suspended outside the boundaries of time and life as you now know it."

Again I questioned her on the premise of the palm tree being of illusionary quality.

She rose, grasped my hand and led me to a nearby palm tree. "This palm tree is a reality to you, is it not?"

"Yes, of course," I answered.

"Listen to me very closely," she said. "This palm tree, like the ocean and the sky, are real within the boundaries of nature. They are a natural existence. However, beyond this reality of nature there is a far greater natural state, a superior natural state. Some call it super-natural. The super-natural state is one of spirit essence. It is before the formation of form."

The whole concept tickled my sense of humor and I felt the old lady had gone too far with her outrageous thinking.

She was quick to pick up my feeling and turning to me she said, "I can see that you disbelieve me and if you continue to think in such a way, you will be like many others who never see the abundance of personal power that lies dormant within yourself. I am talking about power that would help you correct any undesirable factor in your life."

"I am sorry," I said, "I'm afraid you have lost me somewhere in this conversation. It sounds nonsensical to me."

Her angelic face broke into a smile. "Let me put it this way. That palm tree is what we call a natural phenomenon, is it not?"

"Yes." I replied.

She then asked me to look closely at a huge knotted growth that was on the trunk of the tree. "Is this growth a natural phenomenon also?" she asked again.

I answered, "Yes."

She continued by saying, "Although the tree and the growth are natural in their own right, they are not natural to each other. However, a tree does not have the power to think. It has no personal power, therefore it becomes a victim of nature."

I failed to see her point and was about to question her again when she said, "Patience, young man, patience. All in good time."

Mamma Lila sat in silent meditation for awhile then Jonathan returned from his stroll along the beach. The sky was getting dark. It was time to head back to the Coco Palms.

# CHAPTER 10

THE following morning I met Jonathan at the Coco Palms. I explained to him that the evening's conversation with Mamma Lila had left me so confused that I hadn't slept a wink all night.

"What did she say that disturbed you so much?"

"It's difficult to say. She talked about illusionary values, relating her whole conversation to a palm tree. She spoke of natural versus super-natural. To be quite frank, there was no specific point to her whole talk. It sounded like a riddle, yet for some unknown reason it disturbed me very much."

*Second Chance*

Jonathan looked at me compassionately and said, "I told you that she was a unique person and that she talked in a manner that was not comprehensible to many people. Such a person as Mamma Lila provokes her listeners to experiment with new ideas; this in turn helps break any limitations they have placed on themselves. My advice is, next time you are talking to Mamma Lila, don't listen to her words. Words are only tools that assist us to communicate with each other. The problem is, very often they are contaminated with our past association of them so they control us instead of us controlling them. In short, we become prisoners of our own contaminated thoughts. We become prisoners of our past."

There was no doubt in my mind that what Jonathan had just said contained some validity. "The big question is, how can you think your way out of a self contaminated thought system?" I asked.

"You can't," Jonathan replied.

At this point I felt the whole damn thing was incomprehensible and a feeling of despair ran through me. It sounded to me as if there was no way out of my predicament.

Jonathan was quick to notice. He said, "Without a word spoken, does not the simple smile of a child transcend all language barriers?"

There was a long silence as I tried to ascertain the meaning of his analogy.

"I told you," he said, "that it took courage to find the knowledge you are looking for. Now look at you. You are whimpering like a puppy and see nothing but defeat. Didn't I tell you that one has to learn to *listen* and that *listening* takes you beyond the word to the unbelievable phenomena of HEARING and SEEING.

"HEARING and SEEING are before the contamination. It is hearing with a lucid mind, a mind with no contaminated thoughts blocking your evolutionary progress."

"What you are saying sounds good in theory," I said, "but what practicality does it have in life?"

Jonathan looked at me closely. "Have you ever thought of it this way, Richard, that one person's philosophy can be another's reality?"

"I'm afraid my skepticism does not allow me to believe in such a simplistic theory," I replied. "All your statements," I continued, "are too generalized and can't possibly relate to everyone. It might be applicable if you were more specific in your statements."

Jonathan answered by telling me that when he first met Mamma Lila he had also thought the same as me, that she was very apt to generalize in her statements. "I questioned her about this," Jonathan went on, "and she said, 'Philosophy is a subject that must be spoken in generalizations. This is where true philosophers hold their power. Philosophy, being nothing specific, encompasses more than any of the other sciences or combination of sciences. Trying to put restrictions on philosophy would be like putting the mighty shark in a bathtub.'

"She had continued by saying, 'True philosophy has no rules, regulations or rituals holding it prisoner. It's as free as the trade winds.' She suggested that perhaps some day if I stopped my petty way of thinking I would hear what the trade winds were trying to say.

"At that time her words had baffled me and I protested that a generalization such as 'Everyone in the world likes peanuts', is ridiculous."

"What did she say to that?" I inquired.

"She said I was swimming in a bathtub!"

The thought of Mamma Lila putting Jonathan in his place touched my sense of humor and as usual he joined me in my amusement.

"It's an amazing thing," he said, "there are limitless ways to attain true knowledge, yet no matter how it is done the result is the same. All who find it are very stable, happy people with an insight into something that is beyond our reasoning."

It was a beautiful morning so we decided to go to the beach. When we arrived the sun was hot and had a soothing therapeutic effect on my back, which had ached all night.

As I relaxed on the lounge chair I couldn't help thinking that there were only three days of my vaca-

*Second Chance*

tion left. The thought of returning to New York did not appeal to me at all. I wondered if this would be my last visit to the Hawaiian Islands?

Never before had I felt so strongly that something was happening to me. Something that was confusing yet at the same time fascinating. I felt as though I were on a roller coaster going nowhere. It was a sensation I had never experienced before and was one certainly impossible to explain to anyone.

The sun was hotter now and seemed to immerse me in a blanket of peace. Soon I fell into a deep slumber.

When I awoke, I found to my surprise that I had been sleeping nearly two hours. Jonathan was nowhere in sight and by now the sun was getting too hot. It was a pleasure to cool off in the gentle surf.

I sat in the shade of a nearby tree, watching the children and their parents enjoying themselves. Resting my back against the tree, I started to think about the riddle Mamma Lila had talked about the previous evening.

It appeared to me that Jonathan was quite reluctant to assist me in solving the riddle of the palm tree. When I had asked him about it, he said it was something I had to realize on my own because if he told me the answer, it would be of little value.

There was a movement behind me. Turning, I saw Jonathan holding two glasses of pineapple juice, just what I needed after lying in the hot sun.

## Second
## Chance

My thoughts were again on Mamma Lila and I asked Jonathan how old she was. "All I know is that she told me she was a young child when the Pioneer Inn was being built in 1901," he replied.

It was difficult to believe she was that old. I mentioned this to Jonathan. Smiling, he said, "She is the kind of person who would never harm a living soul and perhaps all the love she has acts as a deterrent against age."

He again mentioned that Mamma Lila was not like us, that she lived in a different reality than most people. "This makes it difficult to grasp what she is saying or perhaps I should say, it makes it difficult to comprehend the meaning behind what she says.

"When I first met Mamma Lila I couldn't for the world of me understand how she knew so much, when she had had absolutely no formal education."

"That's amazing," I said. "Where did she learn her philosophy?"

"She told me that all her knowledge comes from spirit power."

"What did she mean by spirit power?" I asked.

"It's a force that assists you to see greater realities than you now realize exist. In short, it is the reconciliation of the spiritual and psychological sides of life. This reconciliation is where the East meets the West."

"What do you mean where the East meets the

West?"

"The Eastern philosophers have philosophized for centuries about the wonders and mystical powers of the Spiritual Mind. Western psychoanalysts insist on relating problems to the so-called 'little mind'. One side is spiritual and talks about the intangible, illusive *Master Mind*. The Western psychoanalyst is basically nonspiritual dealing with the tangible. No one can really understand this until one *sees* that one is talking about a source and the other is talking about a formation of the form the source has taken."

Again Jonathan had come up with some interesting theories and somewhat controversial statements. By this time it was late afternoon and Jonathan said that he had a previous appointment. Before leaving, he mentioned that we had been invited to Mamma Lila's for the following evening. After he had gone, I drifted into a deep and welcomed sleep.

# CHAPTER 11

**I**T was a warm, calm evening and the drive to Mamma Lila's was pleasant. The thought that my vacation was drawing to a close interrupted my contentment when I realized that I had only one day left and that most of it would be spent in travelling.

On arrival at Mamma Lila's I was greeted by Jonathan who told me that Mamma Lila was taking a stroll along the beach. He suggested that we join her. As we walked down the path I could see Mamma Lila wandering along the beach towards us. For some unknown reason I began to have the same mystical feelings I had experienced the first evening I entered Lahaina. This time the feelings were so strong that I experienced panic as my mind raced in circles trying to find a rational explanation, but none came. I had read of encounters with unusual characters who were supposed to have a deeper insight into life—people who possessed knowledge beyond our reasoning. To me, such people were merely imaginative figures drawn from the minds of writers, poets and storytellers. It was unrealistic to think anything else, but now I was beginning to doubt such thoughts.

Mamma Lila greeted Jonathan with her usual graceful embrace, followed by the melodious "Aloha." We sat on the same grassy knoll as before and soon Jonathan was telling us about his intention to visit his son and daughter-in-law on the mainland. Listening to him talk about his family was interesting and I soon began to relax.

In front of us was a sky of brilliant red and orange colors. It was the most breathtaking sight I had ever witnessed. A sensation of intense beauty ran through me and I wished I could share this magnificent scene with my friends in New York.

There was a serenity about the place that neither artist could paint nor writer put to pen. It made me realize the impossibility of sharing such an experience with mere words. I was beginning to realize what Jonathan meant when he said words alone cannot ex-

*Second Chance*

press true meaning.

There was a long silence as we feasted our eyes on the natural grandeur that lay before us. It was my last evening in the islands and there were many questions I felt compelled to ask. Breaking the silence I asked Mamma Lila if she would answer a question that had bothered me since our last meeting.

"Certainly," she replied.

"The other evening when you were talking about the palm tree, you said, 'A tree does not have the power to think. It has no personal power. Therefore it becomes a victim of nature'."

"Yes, that is what I said. Did I not also tell you that the reality that now exists for you is but a reflection of thought?"

"Yes, you did and those words are still meaningless to me."

Mamma Lila looked at me and said, "Unlike the tree, you do have the gift of thought. Learn to use it wisely." She continued by saying, "Thought is a cosmic instrument that keeps life pulsating. Without the gift of thought, life would cease to be. All that you survey comes from the invisible and thought is the link between the invisible and the visible. Thought, young man, is your bridge to the cosmic wisdom that will assist you to SEE the hidden powers that lie within your own consciousness."

"Who taught you your philosophy?" I asked Mamma Lila.

"I had a very wise and beautiful teacher, my kupuna kane -- grandfather. When I was a little girl I would sit for hours as he told me about the mysteries of the universe. He would take me with him on nights such as this and teach me to capture Mana power. I knew my kupuna kane was a very wise person but I didn't realize the precious legacy he was preparing me for at the time."

"I am assuming that by the word legacy you don't mean property or financial gain?"

"No, my kupuna kane left me the greatest legacy of all, *wisdom.*"

"What kind of things did he teach you?"

"He taught me how to live in harmony with the natural phenomena that we are now witnessing."

"But how?" I asked.

Mamma Lila again answered me with the words, "Patience, young man, patience."

Patience was something I had very little of, due to the circumstances in my life. To me, 'patience, young man' was not an answer and I was about to rephrase the same question when Jonathan lifted his finger to his lips to indicate silence. Then in pantomime he moved his lips forming the word *listen.* Suddenly it became apparent to me that Jonathan was right. I wasn't as good a listener as I had thought I was.

Jonathan had expressed this the second day we met

by saying that my enthusiasm to learn was far greater than my enthusiasm to *listen*.

Mamma Lila broke the silence by saying. "The knowledge that my kupuna kane taught me was a gradual process. It took many years to find out what he was trying to get me to SEE. It wasn't until I was seventeen years of age that I finally broke through to the world beyond our senses and found the secret of Mana."

"I remember as if it were yesterday. My kupuna kane cried with joy when the pearl of wisdom was handed to me from the spirits."

"It was only two weeks later that my kupuna kane decided to leave this material reality and join my kupuna wahine -- grandmother -- who had died two years earlier."

As she spoke about her grandfather her face revealed her great love for him. It was obvious that there had been a very close bond between them.

We sat quietly for a moment then I said, "Mamma Lila, please tell me about Mana."

At this point she rose and walked towards the ocean. She stood gazing out towards the sea for a couple of minutes then beckoned me to her. "You asked me to tell you about Mana. Mana, in essence, is love. When digested it opens the door to all cosmic consciousness, bringing miraculous powers in its wake.

"True love is pure spirit power being manifest. The

85

manifestation can take many forms. There is a mother loving her child, a doctor caring for his patient, a father playing with his children, a child with a new puppy, people caring for the less fortunate.

"Love is a positive *feeling* and if people cultivate this feeling in their lives, they will surely free themselves from any unbalanced conditions that surround them.

"Love is not just an idea. Love is a living, breathing essence that the wise can pluck from the air at will and then like a master artist mold it into something beautiful.

"Love, my dear Richard, makes the impossible, possible."

When she stopped talking, an incredible tranquility came over me and before I could say anything Mamma Lila said, "Look within yourself for the answer you seek." With these words she stepped forward and embraced me saying, "It is time to part and if it be written, we will meet again. Until then, Aloha, my young friend, and may God be with you."

Leaving Mamma Lila on the beach, Jonathan and I walked towards our cars. Turning to Jonathan I thanked him for the hospitable way he and Mamma Lila had treated me during my vacation. "It has been the most uplifting and interesting experience of my life. There is no way I can say that I understand your philosophy, however, you have given me a lot of food for thought."

Jonathan smiled at my words as he extended his hand and the final Aloha was said.

# CHAPTER 12

THE flight back to New York seemed timeless as I recalled my experiences with Jonathan and Mamma Lila. When we landed at Kennedy Airport I was pleasantly surprised. Contrary to my thinking, New York was not the dismal place I had expected. I was delighted to see the familiar faces of a few friends who had come to the airport to meet me. They were anxious to hear all about my vacation in the Hawaiian Islands. When I told them of my strange encounters with Jonathan and Mamma Lila, there was a sense of disbelief and the more I talked about it the more unbelievable the story sounded, even to me. However unbelievable a story it was, the most dramatic event was still to come.

Five days later, I reported to the clinic for my regular check-up. Upon entering the office, the old feelings were with me again. After the usual series of tests I was told that I would be hearing the results from them in a few days.

Two days later, to my surprise, I was asked to report to the clinic for a new set of tests. Immediately my imagination ran wild as I tried to ascertain how serious my situation really was. I phoned my friend, Dr. Johnston, to see if he could shed any light on why I needed to take another set of tests.

"I'm sorry," said the nurse, "Dr. Johnston is on vacation and won't be back for another week. I'm afraid we have no report from the clinic as yet, but don't worry, Mr. Sullivan, I am sure it is nothing too serious."

All night I paced the floor in dreaded fear. The next morning my heart was palpitating as I entered the clinic. "Good morning," I said, "I am Mr. Sullivan and I was told to report for another set of tests."

The receptionist thumbed through a few papers. "Oh yes, Mr. Sullivan. The doctor will see you in a few minutes."

The next few minutes were like days, as the clock on the wall ticked away. Finally the receptionist called my name and I was shown into the doctor's office.

"Good morning, Mr. Sullivan. Please be seated." There was a silence as I looked into the eyes of the man who would pass sentence on me.

"Mr. Sullivan, the reason I asked you to come here today is because there is something rather difficult to explain. All your tests show negative results. To be frank with you, I have no explanation. It appears all the cancer has simply vanished."

I stood in absolute shock. Tears ran down my cheeks as I thanked God for a second chance. The doctor rambled on but I heard nothing of what he was saying. Jonathan was right. There was an answer to everything. I knew now that I had found the riddle of the palm tree. Mamma Lila in her infinite wisdom had shown me something of great beauty and I knew in my heart that I must return to Hawaii and perhaps find that pearl of wisdom she spoke of.

# In Quest of the Pearl

Richard searches for a deeper understanding of his miraculous healing in the sequel to **SECOND CHANCE**, entitled **IN QUEST OF THE PEARL**. He returns to Maui where he reunites with Jonathan and Mamma Lila. Once again, he finds their wisdom intellectually contradictory, but most intriguing.

**IN QUEST OF THE PEARL**, like **SECOND CHANCE**, is a simply told, very moving story bringing the reader into a world of soft tropical beauty, where undiscovered depths of feeling are waiting to be found.

**IN QUEST OF THE PEARL** is available from your local bookstore or may be ordered directly from the publisher at the following address:

**Duval-Bibb Publishing Co.**
P.O. Box 23704
Tampa, Florida 33623 U.S.A.
(813) 870-1970